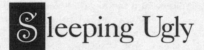

Sleeping Ugly

By Howie Dewin

■SCHOLASTIC

Scholastic Children's Books
Commonwealth House, 1-19 New Oxford Street
London WC1A 1NU, UK
a division of Scholastic Ltd
London ~ New York ~ Toronto ~ Sydney ~ Auckland
Mexico City ~ New Delhi ~ Hong Kong

First published in paperback in the USA by Scholastic Inc., 2004
First published in paperback in the UK by Scholastic Ltd, 2004

Shrek is a registered trademark of DreamWorks L.L.C.
Shrek 2 TM and © 2004 DreamWorks L.L.C.

ISBN 0 439 96311 7

Printed and bound by AIT Nørhaven A/S, Denmark

2 4 6 8 10 9 7 5 3 1

ONE

Ph-ff-l-aaa-t! An explosion of sound and smell poured from Shrek's outhouse just as the air filled with small white balls. *Pop! Pop! Pop! Pop!* They struck the front of Shrek's house.

"Oh, now that's just rude!" snapped Donkey as Shrek strolled from the outhouse.

"Well, excuse me, Donkey," Shrek exclaimed, "but it's my outhouse and it's my house and it's my swamp! I'm an ogre and I'll do as I—"

Pop! Pop! Pop! More white balls sailed by.

"What the—" Shrek grabbed his ear and pulled

1

out a breadcrumb. "Hansel and Gretel again!" he growled.

"See? That's what I'm talking about. But what can you do? The kids love you, Shrek," said Donkey with a nod to the young fairy-tale creatures at the swamp's edge.

"They've got a funny way of showing it!" Shrek grumbled.

"Well," laughed Donkey, "that's kids! The more they tease you, the more they like you."

Shrek shook his head. He had always loved the privacy of his mucky wet swamp. But that all changed after he saved the fairy-tale creatures from the nasty Lord Farquaad. The creatures had moved out of the swamp after Farquaad had left but they wouldn't stop visiting. Shrek was their hero and they liked spending time in his swamp.

"They just never go away," Shrek mumbled.

"I know." Donkey smiled. "It's really hard to be an amazing superstar!"

Shrek groaned and walked towards his house where his lovely green wife, Fiona, waited.

"What's up, Shrek?" shouted a little gnome.

"Ogres rock!" yelled a girl with blonde plaits.

Pop! Pop! A breadcrumb flew up Donkey's nose.

"Okay! That's it!" Donkey shouted through a plugged nose. He charged the gang of children. They screamed and scattered.

Fiona smiled at Shrek when he reached the house.

"Kids!" Shrek grumbled.

"Maybe if we actually invited them in . . . you know? Be a little less cranky? Then they wouldn't think it was so exciting to sneak up on you," Fiona gently suggested.

"I like being cranky," Shrek said.

In the forest, Donkey had cornered the kids.

"Pretty sweet moves for stumpy little donkey legs, eh?" he bragged.

"We didn't mean to hit you, Donkey!" a little bear replied.

"Maybe not," Donkey snorted, "but you did. And besides, Shrek doesn't like it much when you do it to him either."

A little fairy flew forwards. "We're just messing around!"

"We think Shrek's cool!" cried a little gingerbread boy.

"Yeah!" a little kitten purred. "We just want to hang out with him."

Donkey studied the kids. He knew they were just being kids. But he also knew his friend Shrek was getting annoyed and it wasn't a good idea to get an ogre annoyed.

"Okay," Donkey said. "How about this. I'll smooth it over with Shrek and let you come into the yard. *But*, you *have* to be *quiet*. So, I'll read a story and you listen. That way, you see Shrek and Fiona up close but you don't make any noise."

The little fairy flew forwards again. "How come he won't just play with us?"

"What you have to try to understand is," Donkey answered, "Shrek is like an onion. . ."

The little fairy smirked. "What's that supposed to mean then?"

Donkey grimaced. He'd never been sure what Shrek had meant by that. "Look," he said. "Is it yes or no? You want to hear a story or not?"

The kids cheered and screamed, "YES!"

"And after the story, do you promise you will all go home?" he continued. The children nodded. Donkey took a deep breath. This was going to be a little tricky, he thought. It was a brilliant plan but Shrek might not exactly see it that way.

When they got to the clearing where Shrek's house stood, Donkey stopped. "Wait here," he told the children. "I'll give you the nod when it's time to come into the yard."

The children giggled as Donkey headed towards Shrek's front door.

"Did you handle the little fairy rats?" Shrek asked

Donkey when he arrived.

"Oh – yeah. Sure. No problem . . . but, well, you know – I've been thinkin', Shrek. . ."

The ogre raised an eyebrow. He smelled trouble.

"Well, I was just thinkin' . . . it might be a good idea to actually invite them in. Then it wouldn't seem like such a challenge to them, you know?"

"You sound like Fiona," Shrek said as he furrowed his brow. "I'll tell you what I told her. Absolutely not. Once I say yes, they'll *never* go away."

Donkey looked away nervously but kept talking. "I'll tell you what I was thinking – a neighbourhood story hour! How brilliant is that? It's calm and quiet and when the story is over, they go home!"

"First of all, Donkey, this is not a neighbourhood, it's my swamp. And second of all – what's this?"

Shrek's eyes were wide with surprise. A crowd of young creatures had appeared behind Donkey. There were Hansel and Gretel, three little blind baby mice, the gingerbread boy and two tiny fairies, three little kittens without mittens, a long-nosed boy, an odd extra-small gnome and one baby bear.

"Well, uh," Donkey stuttered, "like I said earlier – did I mention I've *already* told the children about the neighbourhood story hour?"

The children cheered and jumped around Shrek as Shrek bellowed, "Donkey!"

"It's cool, Shrek," Donkey said as he ran towards the outhouse. "It's all on me! I'm the storyteller. All you have to do is hang out and be Shrek-like!"

Donkey came out of the outhouse carrying the *Great Big Book of Fairy Tales* that Shrek used for toilet paper.

"You're going to read them a *fairy tale!*" Shrek cried.

"Well, only if I can find one that still has all its pages," Donkey mumbled as he flipped through the book with his hoof.

"I *hate* fairy tales!" Shrek shouted.

The children watched their hero in amazement. No matter what he said or did, they smiled and giggled.

The brave little fairy flew forwards and spoke

nervously. "If you don't want to read a story," the fairy tittered, "then maybe you want to play hide-and-seek with us instead!"

The children cheered loudly and began jumping up and down and pulling on Shrek's arms.

"No!" Shrek exclaimed in horror. "No hide-and-seek! Donkey, do something! Get them off me! Read the story!"

"Sit down!" Donkey shouted in a voice that even surprised him. The children fell silent and sat down in an instant.

Shrek rubbed his face and groaned. Donkey was always getting him into something and now he'd really done it!

"Well, it looks like this one is the only one that has all the pages," Donkey said as he smiled at Shrek.

"Which one?" Hansel asked.

"Sleeping Beauty," Donkey announced.

The children let out a cheer and waited expectantly for the story to begin.

Once upon a time, a peaceful and lovely kingdom was ruled by a very handsome and good king named Stephen and his beautiful and kind wife, Queen Anne.

Nearby, King Louis ruled another fine kingdom filled with more really good-looking and nice people. King Louis had a young son named Prince Philip.

Long ago, the Kings had made a promise to each other that one day their children would marry and the two wonderful kingdoms would become one. So, it was a joyous moment when King Stephen and Queen Anne announced the birth of their daughter, Rose. King

Stephen declared a great celebration to introduce Philip and Rose. Ladies and knights dressed in their finest silks, and twelve gilded carriages brought King Louis, Prince Philip and their attendants to Princess Rose's castle.

Shrek groaned. He covered his ears. He was starting to think he'd rather play hide-and-seek than listen to a fairy tale. They were always full of beautiful people and perfect kingdoms and they weren't very nice when it came to ogres. He looked at the children listening to Donkey. They weren't exactly "fairy-tale beautiful" either, he thought. But Donkey kept reading.

As the people cheered, a shimmering light with the colours of the rainbow filled the great hall. Three good fairies, Molly, Blossom and Wanda, appeared. They flew to the baby's side and gazed at her sweetness.

The first fairy, Molly, flicked her wand and gave the Princess the gift of extraordinary beauty.

The second fairy, Blossom, sprinkled dust from her wand onto the slumbering babe and proclaimed the child to have an amazing gift for music.

Just as the third fairy was about to offer her gift, the castle filled with a thick, choking black smoke. As the smoke faded, they saw before them the horribly evil but quite beautiful fairy, Egoella.

"Someone forgot to invite me," she growled, "even though I'm the finest-looking fairy by far!" The air now filled with a glowing green light.

The Kings and Queen trembled with fear. The people shuddered. The dark fairy with her perfect nose, porcelain skin and pearly-white teeth was known for her great vanity and for her terrible deeds.

"Though I was not invited, I have still brought a gift!" she cried.

The three good fairies gasped at the thought of a gift from Egoella.

The evil fairy lifted her wand and spoke quietly to the innocent baby:

"Enjoy your gifts of song and beauty
Since you won't live long as a musical cutie.
Before your sixteenth birthday, you'll say goodbye
When you prick your finger on a spindle and DIE!"

The people screamed and cried. Queen Anne nearly fainted. King Stephen's fine, strong features lit with anger—

"Stop!" Shrek shouted. "I can't stand it!"

The children gasped.

"I can't stop now," Donkey protested quickly. "It's just getting good."

"I HATE fairy tales!" Shrek bellowed. "Give me that book!"

Donkey jumped back as Shrek's big hands ripped the pages into tiny bits.

"But what happens next?" whined Gretel.

"Yeah!" the other children joined in. "What about Philip and Rose?"

Donkey frowned at Shrek. "Now what are you going to do?"

The children were starting to shout. The kittens began pawing at Shrek's leg.

"Hide-and-seek!" cried one of the fairies, and the children fell on Shrek.

"No! No! No!" Shrek pleaded. "Get off me! All right! I'll finish the story but I'll do it *my* way!"

The children cried out in glee as they climbed on Shrek. Donkey couldn't believe his ears. His plan was even more brilliant than he had thought.

"SIT DOWN!" Shrek thundered. "I can't hear myself think."

The children fell to the ground in silence. They leaned forward and waited for the great Shrek to begin. Shrek scratched himself, took a long deep breath, and continued the story . . . his way.

As the beautiful people screamed and fainted and basically proved themselves to be of absolutely no help whatsoever – the three oddly pudgy little bulbous-nosed fairies hid themselves away behind a great pillar and began to prepare their victory plan. . .

THREE

"This is bad," cried Molly, and she mopped her brow. She always sweated a lot when she was nervous.

"Yes," Blossom agreed. "It's bad but that's why it's f-fortunate we're f-fairies." Molly reached over and dabbed Blossom's chin where the spit had gathered. Blossom's buckteeth made it hard for her to keep the spit on the inside of her mouth.

"Try not to say too many 'f' words, honey," Molly said. "It just makes for more spit."

"That's a f-fact!" Blossom agreed, and the spit landed on Wanda's nose.

Wanda wiped her face and said, "We just have to find a way to protect her until she's sixteen." Molly and Blossom flinched at the sound of Wanda's voice. Normally, it was just a little high-pitched. But when she got excited, she sounded like a million and two mosquitoes all buzzing at the same time.

"We could take the Princess deep into the woods and stay there for sixteen years, living simply and without magic to be extra sure no one would notice anything unusual," Molly said. She licked the sweat off her upper lip.

"Boring!" Wanda screeched.

"F-frightening!" Blossom spat. "I, f-for one, am a f-fast-paced city f-fairy. Can't we f-find a f-formula for def-fending her here?"

Wanda wiped her face again and said, "I still have my spell. What if I secretly reverse your two spells so she's not beautiful and she can't sing?"

Molly and Blossom were puzzled.

"Yes!" squealed Wanda. "That's it! We'll move to the

other side of the kingdom with an ugly little baby who cries like a sick otter! No one will ever suspect!"

Molly stopped sweating.

Blossom said, "Fabulous!" and barely spat at all.

The three fairies chased after the King and Queen, who were heading to their private quarters.

Molly tapped the Queen on the shoulder and said, "Your Highness?"

The Queen's face was etched with sadness. Molly felt a bead of sweat forming on her brow. But she took a deep breath and said, "You must trust us. Go now. We will keep her safe."

The King and Queen knew the fairies were filled with goodness. So the Queen carefully placed her daughter in Molly's arms and left with the King.

Wanda pulled out her wand and whispered:

"You were going to be beautiful and sing like a bird
But Egoella appeared, chanting terrible words,
So now you must hide and though it's absurd,

You'll look like a beastie and sound like a nerd."

In an instant, the beautiful baby transformed into a funny-looking, bulgy-eyed little thing with a wail that made Wanda's voice sound like a nightingale.

The three fairies gasped at the sight.

"I guess we'd b-better go and find a new place to live now," Molly stuttered.

"On the f-funky side of town," Blossom agreed.

The three were just about to take flight when the air around them filled with sparkling green dust.

"Hold up!" cried a stout little fairy in a uniform.

"Oh, great," sighed Wanda. "My parole officer . . . Officer."

"You're a f-felon?" gasped Blossom.

"It was just a little spelling mistake – a long time ago," Wanda screeched. "One little King that no one has ever heard of – so okay, I turned him into a rock."

"And now," Officer snapped, "you've screwed up again!"

"What?" screeched Wanda.

"You just used a final spell and left no room for a happy ending! I could write you up seven ways from Sunday!" she shouted.

The three fairies stared dumbly.

"Do I have to spell it out for you?" Officer grunted. "You just used your last spell to turn the Princess ugly. But there's no out, no kiss, no end to the ugly. What happens if she does run into a spinning wheel? How does that get fixed?"

The fairies gasped. Officer was right. They'd really messed up!

"F-forgive us!" Blossom begged. "This has to be f-fixed!" Spit landed on Officer.

"Gross," Officer said and wiped her face.

"You have to help us!" Molly cried.

Officer stared at the three fairies and shook her head.

"The things I do. . ." she muttered. "Okay. I'll authorize one more spell. But it's mine! And that means I'm moving in — for the next sixteen years — and I want my own bedroom!"

The fairies nodded in agreement. Officer looked at
the Princess and said:

"If that spinning-wheel business comes to pass,
Don't worry about the curse — it won't last.
You'll sleep for a while but when you arise
You'll — sing-really-really-good-and-be-a-sight-for-sore-eyes."

Officer rushed through the end bit because she
knew she'd messed up the rhythm of her rhyme. But
she decided to ignore it and lifted her wand to set the
spell. Wanda grabbed her arm.

"Okay," snapped Officer, "so it's not a great poem
but it'll do!"

"No!" cried Wanda. "What if there is no spinning
wheel and she gets to her sixteenth birthday but she's
still ugly and sounds like a toad?"

Officer thought about it long and hard. Then she
shook her head. "I can't figure out how to make that

rhyme. This will have to do!"

She lifted her wand and the spell was cast.

FOUR

Donkey smiled at the children and shuffled over to whisper to Shrek.

"Why are you changing the story so much, Shrek? The kids like the one they know."

"Who's changing the story?" Shrek snapped. "This is how it happened."

Donkey shook his head. "Oh, really? That's not the way I remember it. . . I mean, I'm as willing as the next donkey to accept a few differences here and there but I definitely don't remember any parole officer!"

"Okay, Donkey," Shrek grinned. "Then let's just say

I'm taking *artistic lices.*"

"I believe that's *licence,*" Donkey corrected him.

"I know that. I was making an ogre joke." Shrek smiled, pleased with himself.

"Yeah. Sure. Whatever," Donkey mumbled as he returned to his seat.

"What happened next, Shrek?" the little bear asked.

Shrek scratched his head and continued.

Years passed and the four fairies raised Princess Rose to be a sweet, bulgy-eyed, flat-nosed young lady. But they never told her who she was for fear she might accidentally reveal her identity to the wrong person. So, they spent their days and nights in an enormous loft above a Chinese restaurant on the funkiest corner in the kingdom. Rose loved to lean out of the window and listen to the street kids shout out their songs and poetry. She longed to join them but no one ever wanted to play with her. Her face was a big enough problem when it came to making friends, but once she opened her mouth there was no hope. She sounded like a cross between Kermit the frog and Louis Armstrong.

So she spent most of her time with her beloved fairies. They wore themselves out trying to entertain her without their magic. They were afraid of doing anything that might draw attention to them. As every good fairy knew, magic wasn't always predictable and even the best fairy couldn't always control what might happen when a spell was cast. So the fairies had decided long ago that it would be safer to live without it.

On the eve of her sixteenth birthday, the air in the loft nearly buzzed with excitement.

"F-finally!" Blossom spewed. "We will f-finally stop f-fretting and f-focusing on spinning wheels!"

"Yes," Wanda squeaked, "but we won't have Rose anymore, either. And tonight we must tell her who she really is and why she has lived with us all these years."

"There's so much to do before we deliver her to the King and Queen tomorrow."

"If they want her," Officer whispered, and she looked

over at the peculiar Princess. "I should have tried harder to come up with a rhyme. Now she'll always be . . . unusual looking."

"F-fiddlesticks," Blossom spat.

"Don't beat yourself up," Molly agreed.

But the four fairies were all thinking the same thing: what would the King and Queen think when they saw their rearranged daughter? The good news was that the fairies had kept her safe. The bad news was that they couldn't reverse the ugly.

"Let's throw a big party!" whispered Wanda.

"And let's make it a surprise!" agreed Molly.

"Rose," Officer called, "would you mind running a few errands?"

Rose smiled sweetly even though her teeth were a bit confused and unruly. "Sure," she croaked.

The fairies quickly made a list that would send the Princess to the apothecary, the butcher, the glass-blower, the stone-cutter, the cobbler and the one-shilling shop.

"This is a long list," Rose grunted with a smile.

"No hurry, dear," Wanda said. She helped the Princess on with her jacket.

"F-feel f-free to dawdle," Blossom chirped.

Rose gave the fairies an odd glance and tripped out of the door.

"Okay!" barked Officer as the door clicked shut. "Shake a leg! We have a party to plan!"

FIVE

Princess Rose opened the door of her building and stepped onto the pavement with her eyes on the sky. It was a beautiful day. The sky was blue. The birds were singing. And the fairies had let her go out on her own. That didn't happen very often. She could feel the rhythm of the street come up through her very large feet. Her legs carried her along in a bebop beat. Soon, as often happened, she started hearing rhyming words in her head.

The fairies had always told her she wasn't musical. Maybe that was true. She couldn't sing a note and what she heard in her head wasn't really a song. But she definitely had rhythm and a hard-driving beat.

"You can call me Rose 'cause that's my name.
They say I'm a princess but I think that's lame.
Never seen a princess with a face like mine
But that's okay with me 'cause I look just fine."

Rose smiled. She liked her rhyme and the make-believe of being a princess. But she also smiled because what she said was true. She really did think she looked just fine. It wasn't important that other children had always kept their distance. She had the fairies and the little animals she befriended.

Just then, a mouse skittered across her path and looked up at Rose.

"Hey, little thing, don't be afraid," she croaked. The mouse stopped and cocked its head at the curious sound of her voice. Rose reached down and stroked its head before continuing happily on her way. A pigeon fluttered by. She gargled a giggle and brushed its tail feathers gently.

"It's a beautiful day and I'm outta the house,
Got my crew here with me, a pigeon and a mouse.
Don't ask me what I'd wish for if I had to make a wish
'Cause there's nothin' else I want 'cept my true love Prince's kis-h."

"Well, if I can't make it rhyme, I must not want it that badly!" She laughed as she talked to the pigeon.

Little did Rose know, the pigeon was not the only one listening to her bebop, hip-hop rhymes. Just around the corner stood a tall, skinny young man. His skin was bumpy and his nose and ears stuck out too far. He had a green streak in his hair and his clothes were a mess. But anyone who looked at him knew he was happy with himself. He walked with confidence. He didn't question who he was.

However, at this moment, he didn't move at all. He was too stunned and amazed by the voice and the words floating in the air around him. He loved the rhythm and rhyme. He loved the soulful laughter. He loved the unique voice. Whoever was speaking had stolen his heart.

He took a deep breath and stepped around the corner. He and Rose were face to face. Big nose to big nose, they stared at each other.

Rose didn't understand why her knees felt like jelly. It wasn't an experience she'd ever felt before.

The young man let out a soft gasp. He'd never seen anything so lovely. He knew this was the girl of his dreams.

"What's up, my rhyming beauty?" he asked.

"A bright blue sky, Rooty Tooty," she answered, still trying to figure out why she couldn't stop staring at the young man's face.

"I've been listening to your rap. You've really got some chops."

"You're very kind to say so. Who are you, my Pops?"

The young man smiled and held out his arm for

Rose to take. "I'm a rhyming, rapping, rhythm machine who happens to think your voice is totally keen."

"It's a pleasure to hear someone talk like I talk. I guess there's no harm if we take a short walk." Rose giggled and took the young man's arm.

The young man laughed and said, "I want to show you all my favourite places, the river, the stable, the great carriage races."

Rose's eyes widened. She started to feel as if she were floating. "Is it possible what you have told me is true? Because you just named all my favourites, too."

Rose and the young man took off down the street. They spent the day matching each other's rhymes. They threw rocks in the river, talked to the horses and cheered the beautiful carriages as they raced around the track.

When they left the races, Rose realized she still didn't know the young man's name. So she said, "I feel I know you, we're so much the same, but strangely enough, I don't know your name!"

The young man smiled and took Rose's hand.

"I got a name, that's for sure, folks call me Little Phil.
But say that I'm your Prince and I'll say, 'My heart be still!'
For if you do, then when we kiss (and I promise that we will)
We'll be 'happy ever after' and life will be a thrill!"

Rose swooned. Now she understood everything she had been feeling. She was in love! The world was spinning faster than ever before. She looked to the sky and laughed. That's when she realized the sun was nearly setting. Suddenly she remembered her errands and how many times the fairies had warned her not to talk to strangers. She froze in her tracks. Phil was startled by the sudden change.

"What's this?" he asked.

Rose pulled away from him. She wrote her address on a piece of paper. Then she wrote TONIGHT. 7:30 pm. She put the paper in his hand and said:

"Don't ask me what I'd wish for,
or the thing I always miss
'Cause I'd have to tell you truthfully,
it's my true love Prince's kiss."

"Psst! Donkey!" Shrek pulled Donkey out of his romantic daydream.

Donkey hurried over to Shrek. "That was very, very nice, Shrek."

"You don't think it was too mushy?"

"Definitely not. Very, very nice. But then again, I'm a romantic."

Shrek glanced at the little faces waiting for the rest of the story.

"What about the evil fairy?" demanded Hansel. "I want some action!"

"Yeah! Blow something up!" the little gnome shouted.

"When does the kiss happen?" Gretel asked.

"Yeah!" the three blind baby mice squeaked.

"It's a tough crowd," Donkey muttered. "Better switch it up, Shrek."

Shrek nodded.

"Back to the story," he said loudly.

Preparations at the castle were under way. The King and Queen had waited sixteen years for this day. They planned a huge celebration. The great hall was filled with colourful banners. Ladies and knights were dressed in their finest clothes.

King Stephen stood on the grand staircase of the great hall. He watched long tables being set for the feast.

King Louis entered the hall.

"Louis!" King Stephen shouted. "The day has arrived at last!"

Louis looked oddly nervous and replied, "We must

talk, Stephen."

"Yes! There's so much good news!" King Stephen agreed.

King Louis took a deep breath and said, "Uh, well, it—"

"Use the finest silver and gold," Stephen called to his staff.

"Uh, I don't know how to say this to you," Louis continued. "Well, as you know – the Prince did not exactly grow up like we expected—"

"Break open all the wine!" Stephen announced.

King Louis realized King Stephen wasn't listening at all. He decided he should quickly confess everything. "Prince Philip, it seems, I'm afraid, well, as of today, he has fallen in love with someone else!"

"In love! In love!" King Stephen laughed loudly. "It's wonderful to be in love!"

"We'll be 'happy ever after' and life will be a thrill!" King Louis said. "He chants that – over and over – ever since he fell in love!"

"Action!" Hansel suddenly interrupted Shrek. "Where's the action?"

"All right!" Shrek shouted back. "You want action? I'll give you action!"

Bang! Crash! Clang! Things were not so happy at the castle of the evil fairy Egoella.

"WHY HAS NO ONE FOUND THE GIRL?" she screeched to her army of evil trolls. "SIXTEEN YEARS AND NOTHING?" She scratched the sky with her long fingernails. Then she stopped to admire her reflection in her mirror before screaming, "I BANISH ALL OF YOU!"

Suddenly, the floor beneath the trolls gave way. They screamed in terror and plunged into secret underground fiery rivers. Egoella laughed wickedly. She grabbed the big black bird that perched next to her. "You!" she growled. "You have four hours to find the Princess or the same will happen to you!"

The raven cawed. Then he flew from the castle in search of the Princess.

SEVEN

Back at the loft, the fairies were starting to panic.

"Does this look like a dress to you?" Molly asked. Sweat dripped in a river off her forehead. It landed on a strange clump of fabric sitting on the kitchen table.

"That's a dress?" Officer picked up the fabric. She held what was meant to be the arm but both ends were sewn together.

"F-fairly f-frightening," Blossom spat, "but f-far more f-fabulous than my f-festive f-fruit f-fritters."

The fairies wiped the spit off their faces and studied the black lumps of something that sat on the baking pan. Then they examined the loft and the mess they'd made. There was no dress, no food, and no decorations. Rose would be back soon and there would be no party. Officer sat down in defeat.

"I just don't think we can make a good party without a little magic," Wanda whispered.

One by one, the fairies peeked at one another to see what the others were thinking. Then in an instant they sped to the special box hidden underneath the floorboards. They grabbed their wands and began zapping everything in sight.

"Yee-haw!" Molly shouted. It felt so good to use her magic again.

"Yowsa!" Blossom exclaimed.

"Whoop-tee-doo!" Wanda was so excited that her screech broke three glasses sitting on the worktop.

The noise and sparks also sailed up the chimney. At that very moment, Egoella's wicked raven was flying by. The screech nearly knocked him out of the sky. He swooped down to where the noise began. The windows of the loft were lit up with magical sparks. The raven sat on the window ledge. Right away he recognized the fairies as they zapped the loft into a perfect party place. He also noticed a young girl enter the building from the street below. The raven smiled as much as ravens can. He had found them! Quietly, he flapped his wings and headed back to Egoella with the news.

Rose climbed the stairs to the loft. She had floated home on a cloud of bliss. When she opened the door to the loft, the sight she saw fit her new feelings perfectly. The air shimmered with glitter. Ribbons and bows swooped from door to door. The loft was full of colour and light, and the most beautiful dress she had ever seen floated before her.

Molly, Blossom, Wanda and Officer clasped their hands together and waited for Rose's first words. They were very pleased with their work.

"Oh!" Rose exclaimed. "I'm in LOVE!"

The fairies gasped in horror and surprise. Rose began to dance.

"We'll be 'happy ever after' and life will be a thrill!" she chanted.

The fairies instantly forgot about the party.

"This is a disaster!" Officer roared.

"He's coming here tonight!" Rose exclaimed.

"Tomorrow you're supposed to meet your husband-to-be!" Molly shouted in desperation. "I told you long ago that someday you'd meet your Prince."

"Well, yeah," Rose sputtered, "but you never said it was going to be on a specific day. What are you talking about?"

"Possibly there are a f-few things we f-forgot to mention," Blossom said.

"To the castle!" Wanda screeched. "We'll explain as much as we can on the way."

Rose tried to stop them but the fairies bundled her up and hurried out the door.

"We'll be 'happy ever after' and life will be a thrill!" Rose sobbed again and again as she was pulled from her home.

EIGHT

"Ah-hem!" Donkey was trying to get Shrek's attention.

"What is it, Donkey?" Shrek whispered. "I'm coming to the really exciting part!"

"That's cool. I can appreciate that but I'm a little concerned. . ."

"About what?" Shrek was getting annoyed.

"The happy ending, Shrek! You're still going to have one, right?" He turned away from the children and whispered, "I mean, I know you don't want everything all neat and tidy but you still have to have a happy ending . . . even if it means everybody turns out to be good-looking!"

"It's my story, Donkey! I don't *have* to do anything! Now sit down!" Shrek pointed a big green finger at Donkey.

Donkey sighed and returned to his seat.

"Now," said Shrek, "where were we? Ah, yes. . ."

The fairies used their magic to fly the Princess to the castle. They needed to talk to the King and Queen. They hid Rose away in her old bedroom. Then they stood in the hallway and tried to make a plan.

"Sixteen perfect years," snapped Officer, "and now this! What do we say to her parents?"

"Excuse me, Your Highness? We kept your daughter alive but unfortunately she resembles a frog and oh, yeah, this morning she fell in love with someone we've never met?" Wanda suggested.

"Not!" Officer barked.

"F-first of all," spat Blossom, "I think Molly should talk to them."

"What?" Molly snapped. She was standing in a puddle of sweat. "Why me?"

"Because I'm af-fraid to," Blossom whimpered.

As they argued, a green light glowed from beneath the door.

"Hello?" Officer said when she noticed the light. "What's that?"

"It's a glowing green light," Wanda squeaked. "You know, like the kind Egoella uses when she's doing something really evil."

"AAAUUUGHH!" the fairies screamed. They rushed into the room. Rose was gone!

"Look!" Molly shouted. "That long staircase didn't used to be there!"

"Charge!" shouted Officer. The fairies flew up the winding magic staircase. They flew fast but they couldn't catch the green light.

"Rose!" they shouted. There was no answer.

At last, they reached the top. A big wooden door stood before them. They flung themselves against it.

45

The door swung open.

Their worst nightmare had come true.

Rose lay on the stone floor beneath a spinning wheel. There was a drop of blood on its spindle. The green light floated just outside the window. Suddenly, the light turned into Egoella. She screeched in delighted laughter and vanished.

The fairies fell upon the young Princess and sobbed.

"What have we done?" Molly wailed.

"She's gone!" Wanda shrieked.

"No!" Officer said with a deep breath. "She's not gone! She's sleeping. Now, pull yourselves together!"

"How can we f-fix this?" Blossom sputtered.

"We need some time," Officer announced. "We must put the entire kingdom to sleep until we can set this right. Now, go!"

The fairies obeyed the command. They returned Rose to her room. They laid her gently upon her bed. Then they each raced off in different directions to put the kingdom into a magical sleep.

Molly was in charge of the shopkeepers and townspeople. Officer handled all the children. Blossom made all the animals fall asleep. Wanda was sent to the grand hall to cast a spell on the royal family and court.

As she tapped the Kings and Queen on their heads, she whispered, "I'm sorry." Instantly, they fell asleep. As King Louis fell into a slumber he began to mumble.

"I'm sorry, King Stephen, but the Prince has fallen in love," King Louis said as if he were talking to Rose's father. Then he began to chant, *"We'll be 'happy ever after' and life will be a thrill! We'll be 'happy ever after' and life will be a thrill!"*

Wanda gasped. That was exactly what the Princess had been chanting! Could the Princess have fallen in love with the Prince while she was hanging out on a street corner?

Wanda raced back to the others and told them the news.

"F-f-fantastic!" Blossom spewed.

"He has to kiss her!" Molly cried. "We must find him!"

"He was meeting her at the loft tonight!" Officer shouted. "Charge!"

NINE

The fairies flew so fast they arrived at the loft in minutes. Even so, when they opened the door they knew they hadn't been fast enough. Dishes were broken. Furniture was upside down. The windows were wide open.

"I f-fear Egoella f-found him f-first!" Blossom cried.

"This has not been a good day," Officer moaned.

"You know what this means, don't you?" Molly said. She took off her dress and wrung out the sweat.

"Oooh," Wanda screeched and shattered the last unbroken glass. "We have to go to Egoella's evil and scary castle to find him?"

Molly nodded. The sweat poured down her face. It made it hard for her to talk.

"So much f-for f-fairy-tale endings. . ." Blossom sighed.

"All right," Officer said, "enough wimpy whining! I want to see fairies flying and I want to see it NOW!"

The fairies jumped into the air. They were afraid to disobey. They flew out of the window and straight towards the evil kingdom of Egoella.

"Ooooooh. . ."

Shrek stopped talking. A strange moan filled the air.

"What's that noise?" Shrek asked.

The forest children rolled their eyes. They pointed at Donkey. His head was buried under his legs and his ears were wrapped around his eyes. Shrek shook his head. He tapped Donkey on the shoulder. Donkey slowly pulled an ear away from his right eye and looked up.

"It's bad, Shrek," Donkey said. "It's very bad. I don't

think it's going to work out for the Princess."

"Donkey," Shrek barked, "if you can't take it then go into the house."

"Yeah!" the children cried.

"It's just a stupid fairy tale," said a wooden boy with a big nose.

"Well, thanks a lot," Shrek said. "I thought it was going pretty well."

"You know what I mean," said the boy. "It's a really good story but come on, it's just a story. I would never get scared." At that moment, the boy's nose grew an inch. "Okay, it's a little scary," he confessed, "but keep going!"

The children cheered. Donkey took a deep breath. "I'm cool," he said. "Go ahead, Shrek. I can take it."

The fairies flew and flew. The air grew dark with Egoella's evil smoke. The castle loomed up through the dark mist. One by one, they slipped through the barred windows. Egoella's cackling laugh echoed everywhere.

The fairies darted through rooms. They stayed low to the ground as they zipped down long hallways. They found a dark winding staircase. Down and down it went. At last, they were in the dungeon.

There, they found the Prince. He was tied up and gagged. Without a word, the fairies went to work freeing him.

"Whoop-tee-doo! Who are you?" the Prince exclaimed once he was released.

"Never mind that," Officer said. "You have to kiss a Princess."

"No can do. My heart is true to a girl I met before sunset."

The fairies exchanged glances. Why did he have to rhyme everything?

"Right. That's good," Molly said, "because that's who we're talking about."

The fairies huddled around the Prince. They quickly explained.

"I'll do it! Lead me to it!" the Prince shouted once

52

he understood.

"First," Wanda squeaked, "you'll need your shield of valour and your sword of truth."

The fairies pulled the items from midair. The Prince applauded the magic.

"Cool move!" he said. "Now, watch me groove!"

The Prince dashed from the dungeon on his quest to kiss the Princess.

"Do you think all that rhyming will distract him from his mission?" Officer asked.

"He's a very strange boy," Molly responded.

The fairies nodded in agreement.

TEN

Egoella was fast upon the Prince. She seemed to know he had escaped almost before he had done so.

"Not so fast, you little pimpled Prince!" she screeched.

The Prince scrambled up the cliff from the castle's moat.

"I won't let you kiss her and spoil all my fun!" Egoella exclaimed through gritted teeth.

"You've got no choice, oh evil one!
I'd love to chat but I have to run.
As you can see by the setting sun,

There's little time 'til goodness has won!"

The Prince made a dash for the safety of the forest. Egoella raised her arms and set fire to the trees closest to her. But the Prince was safe within the woods.

"DRAT!" she screamed with her hand around the raven's neck. She shook the bird at the Prince. "You haven't won yet!"

"But I've never met a better bet!" he declared.

Egoella flew over his head as he ran through the forest.

"Stop rhyming!" she screamed.

"Perfect timing!" he shouted and slashed some vines with his sword of truth. Two huge branches fell towards Egoella. She dodged them but lost sight of the Prince. The fairies watched from a distance. They gave each other high fives.

"Aauugh!" Egoella yelped. "How dare you! You have broken one of my perfect teeth! Now you will pay!"

"That Prince is growing on me!" Wanda squealed.

As Egoella screamed, the Prince tunnelled towards the kingdom. He ran through secret passageways he'd played in as a child. In no time, he was at the gates of the Princess's palace.

"Knock, knock, knock, anybody there?
I'm here for my true love, so funky and fair."

The door swung open. There stood Egoella!

"You think I'm stupid? You think you can beat me just like that?"

"I've seen better moves on a twenty-year-old cat!" the Prince answered.

He held up his shield of valour and charged the door.

"I'm not impressed," she shouted. Her powerful evil ripped the shield from his hand. "You look silly with your shield of valour and your sword of truth!"

"They look a lot better than your missing tooth!"

Egoella gasped and covered her mouth in embarrassment. The Prince dashed towards the stairway that led to the Princess's tower. Egoella met him at every turn. But the Prince held her back with his sword. The fairies watched with great concern.

"Would it be f-fair if-f we did him a f-f-few f-favours?" Blossom whispered.

Wanda didn't wait for an answer. She flew at Egoella.

"Take that!" she squeaked. She kicked her little feet in rapid style. In an instant she had tapped out the rest of Egoella's teeth.

"Mmfmffphphllmm," Egoella tried to say. She couldn't make any evil words without her teeth. She couldn't cast any spells (or win any beauty contests).

Molly tapped her wand on the wall behind Egoella. A window appeared.

Blossom flew very close to her and said, "F-farewell, you f-fierce f-fairy!"

Egoella tried to dodge Blossom's flying spit. But instead, she tumbled right out of the window.

"Hooray!" The children were delighted!

Shrek smiled.

"MMFMFMMMMPHPHPHLLLLLMMM!" Egoella
screamed. Then there was a huge splash. Egoella
disappeared into the moat.

At that very moment, the Prince kneeled before the
sleeping Rose. He kissed her on the lips. The fairies
held their breath. Would their spells work?

Rose blinked twice and smiled at her Prince.

"Life will be a thrill!" she whispered.

The King and Queen rushed into the room as the
Prince and Princess embraced. The Queen smiled and
brushed a tear from her eye.

"Finally my daughter. What a beautiful Princess,"
she cried.

"They're a perfect couple," the King whispered.

Shrek looked up. The fuzzy bear and the pointy-
eared gnome were giggling. The pot-bellied dwarf and
the tiny little fairy squealed. Donkey was crying tears

of sheer joy.

Throughout the kingdom, bells tolled joyfully. The Princess was home!

"Yay!" The children cheered and danced.

"Right on!" exclaimed Donkey. "Now that's just beautiful!"

Shrek laughed and said, "And everyone lived happily ever after." And then he looked at Donkey and said, "Okay?"

"Ah, Shrek," Donkey said, "you know I just *love* a happy ending!"